Dear Parents:

Congratulations! Your child is taking
the first steps on an exciting journey.
The destination? Independent reading!

STEP INTO READING® will help your child get there. The program offers
five steps to reading success. Each step includes fun stories and colorful
art or photographs. In addition to original fiction and books with favorite
characters, there are Step into Reading Non-Fiction Readers, Phonics Readers
and Boxed Sets, Sticker Readers, and Comic Readers—a complete literacy
program with something to interest every child.

Learning to Read, Step by Step!

Ready to Read   Preschool–Kindergarten
• big type and easy words • rhyme and rhythm • picture clues
For children who know the alphabet and are eager to
begin reading.

Reading with Help   Preschool–Grade 1
• basic vocabulary • short sentences • simple stories
For children who recognize familiar words and sound out
new words with help.

Reading on Your Own   Grades 1–3
• engaging characters • easy-to-follow plots • popular topics
For children who are ready to read on their own.

Reading Paragraphs   Grades 2–3
• challenging vocabulary • short paragraphs • exciting stories
For newly independent readers who read simple sentences
with confidence.

Ready for Chapters   Grades 2–4
• chapters • longer paragraphs • full-color art
For children who want to take the plunge into chapter books
but still like colorful pictures.

STEP INTO READING® is designed to give every child a successful
reading experience. The grade levels are only guides; children will progress
through the steps at their own speed, developing confidence in their reading.
The F&P Text Level on the back cover serves as another tool to help you
choose the right book for your child.

Remember, a lifetime love of reading starts with a single step!

To Robby, who thought up the idea for this book

Text copyright © 1988 by Jane O'Connor. Cover art and interior illustrations copyright © 1988 by John O'Brien.

All rights reserved. Published in the United States by Random House Children's Books, a division of Penguin Random House LLC, New York.

Step into Reading, Random House, and the Random House colophon are registered trademarks of Penguin Random House LLC.

Visit us on the Web!
StepIntoReading.com
randomhousekids.com

Educators and librarians, for a variety of teaching tools, visit us at
RHTeachersLibrarians.com

Library of Congress Cataloging-in-Publication Data
O'Connor, Jane.
Sir Small and the dragonfly / by Jane O'Connor ; illustrated by John O'Brien.
   p. cm. — (Step into reading. A step 2 book)
Summary: When a dragonfly swoops over the town of Pee Wee and carries Lady Teena away, brave Sir Small rides off on his trusty ant vowing to rescue her.
ISBN 978-0-394-89625-0 (trade) — ISBN 978-0-394-99625-7 (lib. bdg.) —
ISBN 978-0-385-37481-1 (ebook)
[1. Knights and knighthood—Fiction. 2. Size—Fiction.]
I. O'Brien, John, ill. II. Title. III. Series: Step into reading. Step 2 book.
PZ7.O222Si 2003 [E]—dc21   2002153662

Printed in the United States of America 52 51 50 49 48 47 46 45 44 43 42

This book has been officially leveled by using the F&P Text Level Gradient™ Leveling System.

Sir Small
and the
Dragonfly

by Jane O'Connor

illustrated by John O'Brien

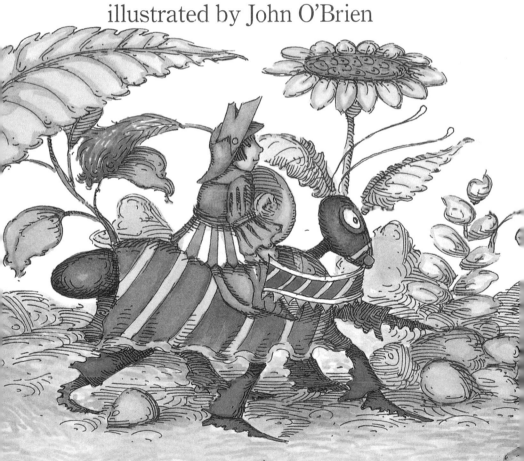

Random House 🏠 New York

Long, long ago
a tiny knight rode
his trusty ant
into the town of Pee Wee.

In Pee Wee
the tallest person was
no taller than a toothpick.
The biggest house was
no bigger than a shoe box.

"This is the town for me!"
said the tiny knight.
"I think I will stay here."
And so he did.

But one day
a dragonfly flew over the town.
'Run for your lives!"
cried the people of Pee Wee.

Lady Teena ran.

Down came the dragonfly.

WHOOSH!

Up went Lady Teena.

"Help! Help!" she shouted.

"The dragonfly has taken
Lady Teena to its cave.
Who can save her?"
asked the king.

The butcher said,
"I am too old."

The baker said,
"I am too fat."

The candlestick maker said,
"I am too scared."

"I am not scared,"
  said the tiny knight.
"You? Who are you?"
  asked the king.
"I am Sir Small.
  I have my sword."
  It was the size of a pin.
"I have my shield."
  It was no bigger
  than a penny.
"And I have my trusty ant."

The king laughed.
"You are even smaller
than we are!"

"I am small,
but I am brave.
I will save Lady Teena."

Sir Small rode to the cave
of the dragonfly.

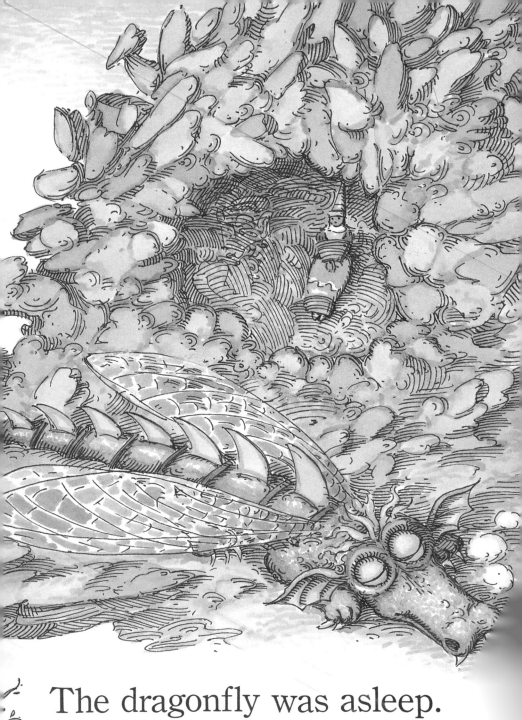

The dragonfly was asleep.

Lucky Sir Small!

"Shh!" he said
to Lady Teena.
Then he cut the ropes.
Lady Teena was free!
"Come with me,"
Sir Small told her.

Lady Teena got on
Sir Small's ant.
Away they rode.
There was no time to lose!

Soon the dragonfly woke up.
Where was the pretty lady?
The dragonfly wanted
her back.

The dragonfly flew
after Sir Small
and Lady Teena.
It came closer and closer.

But Sir Small

was not scared.

He saw a big spider web.

Now he had a plan!

Sir Small rode
behind the web.
"Try and get us!"
he called to the dragonfly.

Down came the dragonfly.
It flew into the web
and was trapped.
That was the end
of the dragonfly!

That night
the people of Pee Wee
had a big party.

Lady Teena
sat with Sir Small.
They were very happy.

The king said,
"Here's to Sir Small.
The smallest—
but bravest—of all!"